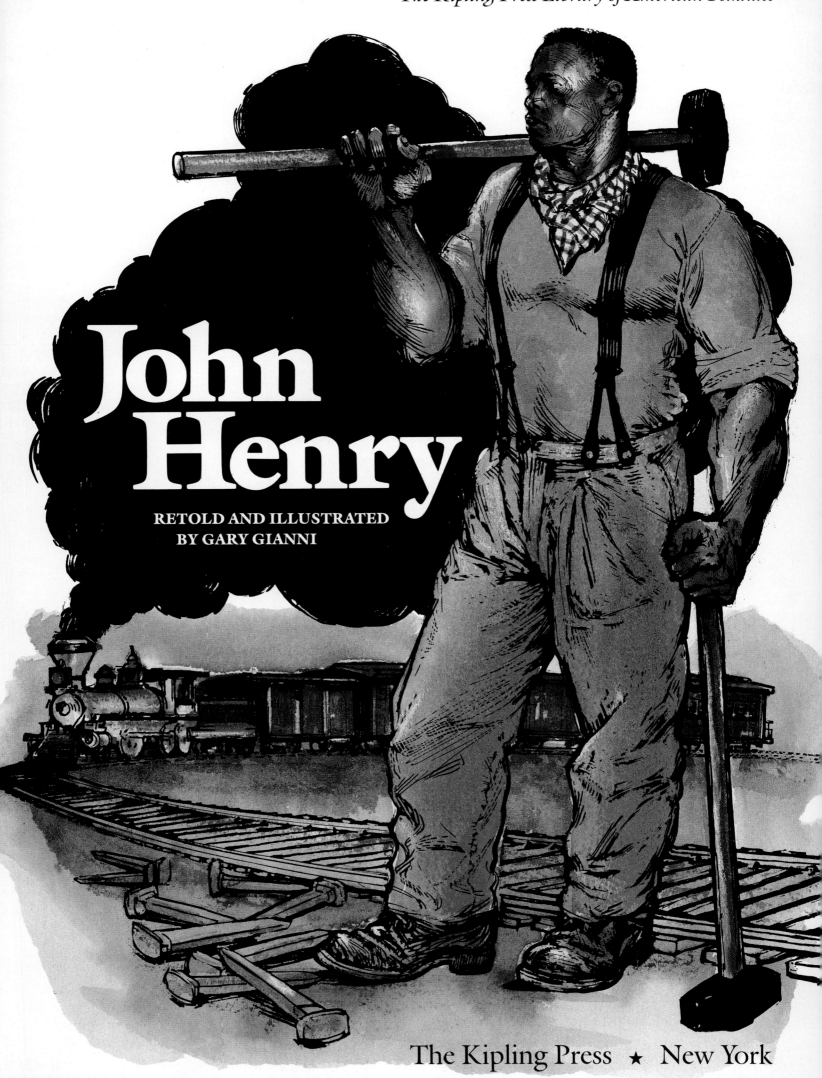

John Henry

**RETOLD AND ILLUSTRATED
BY GARY GIANNI**

The Kipling Press ★ New York

Published by The Kipling Press, Inc.
155 Sixth Avenue, New York, New York 10013
Copyright © 1988 by The Kipling Press
Text Copyright © 1988 by Gary Gianni
Illustrations Copyright © 1988 by Gary Gianni
Book Design by Michael Hortens
All Rights Reserved.

International Standard Book Number: 0-9437-1818-X
Manufactured and Printed in the United States of America

Foreword

We don't know if there really was a man named John Henry who worked as a steel driver and won a contest against a steam drill using two twenty-pound hammers. But it is certainly possible. The contest was supposed to have happened in the 1870s, when the railroads were being built through the mountains of West Virginia. The tunnel through Big Bend Mountain in Summers County, West Virginia, is where John Henry is supposed to have died—after he beat the steam drill. There were people who claimed they knew the real John Henry. Some people who live near Big Bend today say they have seen John Henry's ghost pounding steel in the tunnel.

Even if John Henry's story isn't true, the Big Bend Tunnel is a good place for it. Between 1870 and 1872, workers for the C & O Railway were putting a tunnel through the mountain near the big bend in the Greenbriar River. The contractor, Captain W. R. Johnson, was trying out some of the new power drills. He was probably aware of reports that compared the cost of drilling using machines with the cost of drilling by hand. Drilling by hand was more expensive because it was usually slower than a power drill. It might have been possible, however, for a strong man like John Henry, using *two* hammers, to have beaten a steam drill in a contest. The man with the hammers would have gotten tired, but the early steam drills would probably have broken down after a half hour of nonstop drilling. So there might really have been a John Henry who won a contest against the steam drill.

But why did the story of John Henry become so popular? There are several reasons. For one thing, the railroads were very important to the young country of America at that time. They were the main source for transporting people and goods to the Midwest, which was just being settled, then to the far West. Companies that were building these railroads were eager to be the first ones to reach new settlements. They had to find the quickest way through the eastern mountains—which was often a tunnel. But digging tunnels was extremely dangerous. Many workers were killed. The story of John Henry makes us stop and think about all of the sacrifices that were made in order to build the railroads across America.

John Henry is also popular because he is not afraid to challenge the power of technology. Here is a man who does not believe that machines always do better work than people can do by hand. Sometimes it is more important to preserve human dignity, or a person's faith and pride in his or her own ability.

Also, America loves to see the underdog win, and in this story John Henry is the underdog. He is a black man and a laborer, representing two groups who have often been treated badly by more powerful people. Using only his own strength and endurance, John Henry won out over a machine. In this contest, the underdog wins, even though everyone expected the steam drill to win.

John Henry's race with the steam drill is told in stories and in popular folk ballads. (A ballad is a song that tells a story.) The ballad of "John Henry" was composed by an unknown black singer sometime in the early 1900s. It became popular with black Americans and railroad workers, then with all Americans. John Henry continues to inspire artists, novelists, and playwrights. John Henry's faith in himself, and his boldness in challenging that steam drill his boss thought was so wonderful, makes this one of America's favorite folk stories.

Sandra Dolby Stahl
Associate Professor of Folklore and American
Studies at Indiana University

One hundred and fifty years ago, a terrible storm raged over a tiny town. Rain poured down from huge, angry, black clouds that filled the night sky. Lightning bolts swung down like hammers and cracked mighty oak trees in half, leaving them splintered and smoking. Giants stomping across the earth would have covered their ears at the sound of the booming thunder. Nature was flexing its muscles, and nothing made by humankind could have matched its awesome power.

John Henry was born on that night. He was a fine, handsome baby and he weighed thirty-two pounds. The reason he weighed so much was because he was born with a hammer in his hands.

The wind rattled the windows of the poor little cabin as his mama looked up and declared, "That hammer is a sign. You gonna hear 'bout this child."

His proud daddy said, "I reckon that there storm outside is nature's way of sayin' we got us a natural man here. You gonna hear a heap o' things 'bout John Henry and his hammer."

As he was growing up, John Henry would play for hours with his hammer, pounding sticks into the earth. By the time he was four years old, he was a big, strong boy—big and strong enough to help with the chores.

One day his mama said quietly, "Son, we needs your help. Lord knows how much you likes to

hammer, but I'm afraid you jes gonna have to hang up your hammer for a spell and give your daddy a hand."

John Henry knew how hard his daddy worked chopping cotton and hoeing corn. He loved his parents and always obeyed them. So he carefully hung his hammer on the wall. As he stepped back, he turned to his mama and whispered, "That hammer gonna be the death of me."

As the years rolled by, John Henry grew into a tall, strong young man. He loved to work. He enjoyed doing a job well. His daddy taught him to use the family's simple tools—axes, hoes, shovels, and saws. "A hammer is what I use best," John Henry told his daddy. "The other tools don't seem to fit my hands."

One evening he said to his parents, "You always said I was a natural man, but this work ain't natural to me. I've done all I can do 'round here, so maybe it's time I go find me a natural job."

"I reckon you're right, son," his father said sadly. "It was written in the sky when you was born. You gotta go find your own star." His mama held back her tears, for she knew in her heart her son was right.

The very next morning John Henry set off to find a job. Because of his great size and strength, people were eager to hire him.

His first job was on a plantation working as a cotton picker. John Henry could pick four thousand pounds of cotton a day, but he was not satisfied. He had to move on. The owner pleaded with him to stay, but John Henry told him, "I likes hard work, but this job ain't natural for me and I gotta move on."

Next he hired on as a field hand. One day the foreman sent John Henry out to dig a well. He dug so deep that it took him a day and a night to climb back out of the hole. The foreman was amazed!

A ranch hand laughed, "It would have been a might easier to dig to the bottom of the earth and walk out t'other side!"

"Well, maybe I could have," said John Henry, grinning, "but I was using a shovel, and that ain't natural for me."

That night in the bunkhouse, one of the men began to grumble about the hard work. "It's okay with me," John Henry mused. "A man's gotta have a job, and if he don't like it, it's bound to be hard."

"If I got more money, I'd be happy," the man said.

John Henry replied, "The money don't matter much. All I wants is a hammer in my hand. If I could find work like that, I'd die a happy man."

Years of hard work made John Henry the strongest of men. His arms were as thick as tree trunks, and his shoulders were so wide he could only enter a room sideways.

He was once asked to shoe a horse, and he jumped eagerly at the task. But he was disappointed to find the blacksmith's hammer was much too small for his big hand. "Thought I was gonna get a chance to use a real hammer," he sighed. There was nothing else to do but drive the nails into the horse's hooves with his fist.

That afternoon, John Henry took a stroll along the Mississippi River to ponder his future. As he watched a river steamer pulling into port, an idea came to him. "If I gets me a job on that boat, maybe it'll take me to a new place, a place where there's big jobs needin' big hammers."

The steamer, called the *Diamond Joe*, carried freight from all the river towns down to the seaport. The captain took one look at John Henry and hired him. John Henry loaded the heavy cargo on board the ship and fed wood in the roaring furnace, which powered the *Diamond Joe's* paddle wheel. He was happy to be a crew member on this boat, but he missed using his hammer.

On a summer evening, as the *Diamond Joe* plowed through the river, John Henry sat on the deck, studying the night sky. *I'd like to know which one of them stars belongs to me,* he thought.

Suddenly the steamer lurched. There was a loud scraping along the hull.

"We ran aground!" a crew member cried.

"She's sinking!" yelled the pilot.

"We gotta get her off this sand bar before we capsize," the captain shouted to John Henry.

"Cap'n," hollered John Henry, "if we move all the weight to the back of the ship, maybe I could push the bow up out of the mud." Then John Henry jumped into the river. He found himself chest-high in mud.

"Full steam astern," ordered the captain. John Henry leaned into the bow, pushing and grunting. The ship began to slide out of the stubborn mud.

"Lord Almighty," whispered the pilot. "John Henry's pushing us out!" After one last mighty heave, John Henry felt the boat begin to move on its own.

"She's free! We're floating in the river!" gasped the captain. The passengers and crew cheered as John Henry climbed back aboard.

When the steamboat pulled in for repairs, John Henry went off to explore the town. He found himself on a bluff overlooking a railroad-track site. As he looked down on the workers below, he knew he belonged there.

Some of the men were carrying steel rails and laying them across wooden ties. Other men with hammers in their hands followed them, anchoring the rails to the ties with huge steel spikes. The sound of steel hitting steel rang out like church bells calling John Henry home. "I was born for this," he cried, with tears of joy in his eyes.

"Ever do any steel drivin' before?" asked the track boss.

"Suh, I was born with a hammer in my hand," declared John Henry. "It's as natural to me as breathin'." To prove it, John Henry pushed a pile of tools aside and picked up a twelve-pound hammer. It fit his hand perfectly. He felt like he'd been holding his breath for his whole life, and he let out a deep sigh of relief.

Two men had just finished driving one spike, and had moved down the rail to start the next one. John Henry joined them. The first man struck. *Clang!* The second man struck. *Clang!* In perfect rhythm, John Henry's hammer flashed across the sky and crashed down squarely on the head of the spike, driving it all the way down into the wood. *CLANG!!*

Later, some men swore that *clang* echoed through the valley for a whole minute. Everyone stopped and stared at this mountain of a man.

The foreman broke the silence. "Friend, I've never seen a man hit like that! You got a job!"

And that was how John Henry became a "steel-drivin' man." He carried a hammer in his hand and a song in his heart. He had found his natural place, and his reputation as the best steel driver in America

grew. His daddy had predicted on the night John Henry was born, "You gonna hear a heap o' things 'bout John Henry and his hammer!"

John Henry now felt it was time to get married. So he asked Polly Anne, his childhood sweetheart, for her hand in marriage. When she accepted, he thought his life was complete.

Now, those days, the railroad industry was booming all over the country. One day word came down from West Virginia about a project being started by the C & O Railroad—Big Bend Tunnel. This would be the biggest tunnel ever drilled through a mountain. The C & O called in John Henry to drive steel, and gave him top pay and a company house for him and Polly Anne.

When John Henry saw the huge mountain the
tunnel would go through, his mouth fell open.
"That's a powerful big mountain!" he whistled.

It would be dangerous work drilling the Big Bend
Tunnel, but everyone knew about John Henry's
bravery. If he led the way through the mountain, the
other men would follow.

Sure enough, one day disaster struck.

Work was progressing, and the men were about a
quarter of a mile inside the tunnel when they heard a

low rumble. The rumbling grew louder and closer. The walls and the ground began to tremble.

"CAVE-IN!" somebody screamed. "Run!" It was too late. The roof of the tunnel was only a few feet above the men's heads. The ceiling cracked, and a huge slab of rock broke away. John Henry stepped forward and caught the full weight of the mountain on his back. He gritted his teeth and shuddered. No man on earth could have held up that mountain except John Henry.

The men quickly propped up giant timbers against the rock. Everyone had just enough time to escape before the tunnel collapsed. The dust had barely settled when John Henry said, "Anyone seen my hammer 'round here? I need to get back to work."

More frightening still was the time the men were using explosives to blast through a stubborn rock.

The powder man lit the fuse, then ran to the elevator where the rest of the crew were waiting anxiously to be hoisted to the surface.

"Let's go!" he shouted. But just as the elevator began to rise, its cable snapped. Twenty men were trapped in the cave!

"If that dynamite goes off while we're down here, we'll all be killed!" cried one of the crew.

"I'll put the fuse out," John Henry yelled over his shoulder as he dashed back down the dark tunnel.

He could just make out the fuse burning in the dark, and he knew he'd never reach it in time. Without thinking, he flung his hammer at the hissing spark. With only seconds to spare, the hammer fell with a thud on the last inch of fuse, snuffing out the sputtering flame.

"There's nuthin' John Henry can't do," the men used to say. But his greatest challenge was still to come.

One day when the tunnel was nearly drilled, the owners of the railroad brought out a strange new machine. "It's a steam drill and it can out-drill any sixteen men," the railroad president said proudly. "It's all set up waiting for a test run."

John Henry and his assistant, Bill, were asked for their opinion. "It ain't no good," John Henry stated firmly. "No engine's ever goin' to drive more steel than a man, and Bill and I are aimin' to prove it. Before I let's a steam drill beat me, I'll die with a hammer in my hand."

And so there came about one of the most amazing contests anyone had ever witnessed. The machine and John Henry would drill for a full day, where everyone could see the results measured in stone. John Henry chose a twenty-pound hammer, and Bill checked their drills. Bill was John Henry's shaker. A shaker's job was to hold the drill in place while the steel driver pounded it into the hard rock. Together, John Henry and Bill made a mighty good team.

Early next morning, a thousand people were on hand to see the famous John Henry race against a machine. He kissed his wife for luck, a pistol was fired, and the race was on!

Three men shoveled coal into the boiler of the steam drill. It began to grind away at the hard rock wall. Alongside, John Henry's hammer rose and fell, smacking the drill held by Bill. Through the smoke, Bill could see the machine was pulling ahead.

Hour after hour, John Henry swung his twenty-pound hammer with the same steady rhythm, but the noisy machine was still beating him. When John Henry noticed this, he sang out to Bill, "That old machine is still ahead, but I swear I'll keep swinging till I drop dead. This hammer just ain't gonna do, so reach down there and hand me two!"

Now, with a hammer in each hand, John Henry began to catch up with the machine. "What's that noise?" yelled Bill.

"Ain't nuthin' but my hammers whistlin' in the wind," smiled John Henry.

Great drops of sweat poured off John Henry and sizzled as they rolled down the red-hot handle of his hammer. By late afternoon, the race was neck and

neck. The steam drill labored, but toward evening it began to wheeze and groan. A valve blew out, and scalding steam hissed out of a crack in its boiler. The steady sound of John Henry's hammer grew louder as the steam drill chugged, choked, and finally died.

John Henry had beaten the machine. John Henry had won!

The crowd broke into a roar, but John Henry did not stop. With a dozen more blows, he crashed through the mountain! The tunnel was finished!

John Henry stood for a moment in the fading light at the end of the tunnel. Then he turned and looked back at his cheering friends as they rushed to greet him. Suddenly John Henry wobbled, dropped to his knees, then toppled to the ground.

"Get a doctor," someone cried.

"Ain't no need," John Henry muttered. "I drove more steel than that machine. I finished my job."

No natural man, not even John Henry, had a heart strong enough to stand the strain of this task.

Besides, he loved hard work and he figured he wouldn't find any that could get much harder than this.

A wonderful peace settled over John Henry's face as he looked up at his dear Polly Anne. Then he drew his hammer

up against his chest, let out an enormous sigh, and
closed his eyes. John Henry died with a hammer
in his hands.

John Henry was buried at the head of the Big
Bend Tunnel, and these few words were chiseled on
his tombstone: *"Here lies a steel-drivin' man."*

Today some folks claim John Henry's spirit still
roams the railroad tunnels across the land. They also
say that whenever people pass through a tunnel,
John Henry will be there to protect them.